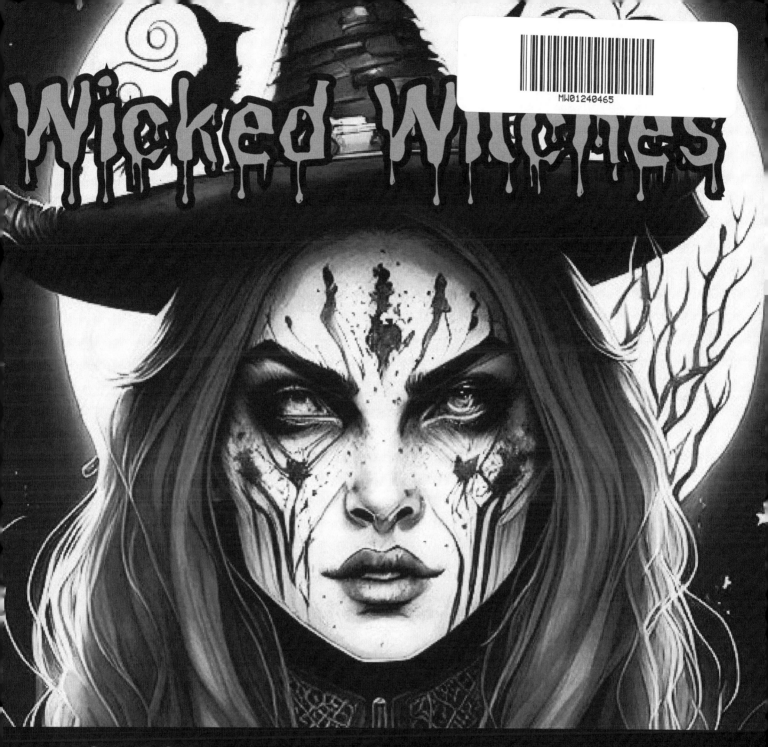

Wicked Witches

HORROR Coloring Book Collection

INFINITE CREATIVITY *Publishing*

We hope you enjoy your book from Infinite Creativity Publishing!

We're writing to ask you a favor - we'd love to get your feedback. We put a lot of work into creating high-quality content & imagery. We love the craft and hope you appreciate it.

Your opinion is super important to us, and we're always looking for ways to improve our products & artwork. So we would be very grateful if you can **please leave us a review on Amazon**! Thank you and have a blessed day.

Also, feel free to visit us at our website available via the QR code below.

PAGE INTENTIONALLY LEFT BLANK

PAGE INTENTIONALLY LEFT BLANK

PAGE INTENTIONALLY LEFT BLANK

PAGE INTENTIONALLY LEFT BLANK

PAGE INTENTIONALLY LEFT BLANK

PAGE INTENTIONALLY LEFT BLANK

PAGE INTENTIONALLY LEFT BLANK

PAGE INTENTIONALLY LEFT BLANK

PAGE INTENTIONALLY LEFT BLANK

PAGE INTENTIONALLY LEFT BLANK

PAGE INTENTIONALLY LEFT BLANK

PAGE INTENTIONALLY LEFT BLANK

PAGE INTENTIONALLY LEFT BLANK

PAGE INTENTIONALLY LEFT BLANK

PAGE INTENTIONALLY LEFT BLANK

PAGE INTENTIONALLY LEFT BLANK

PAGE INTENTIONALLY LEFT BLANK

PAGE INTENTIONALLY LEFT BLANK

PAGE INTENTIONALLY LEFT BLANK

PAGE INTENTIONALLY LEFT BLANK

PAGE INTENTIONALLY LEFT BLANK

PAGE INTENTIONALLY LEFT BLANK

PAGE INTENTIONALLY LEFT BLANK

PAGE INTENTIONALLY LEFT BLANK

PAGE INTENTIONALLY LEFT BLANK

PAGE INTENTIONALLY LEFT BLANK

PAGE INTENTIONALLY LEFT BLANK

PAGE INTENTIONALLY LEFT BLANK

PAGE INTENTIONALLY LEFT BLANK

PAGE INTENTIONALLY LEFT BLANK

PAGE INTENTIONALLY LEFT BLANK

PAGE INTENTIONALLY LEFT BLANK

PAGE INTENTIONALLY LEFT BLANK

PAGE INTENTIONALLY LEFT BLANK

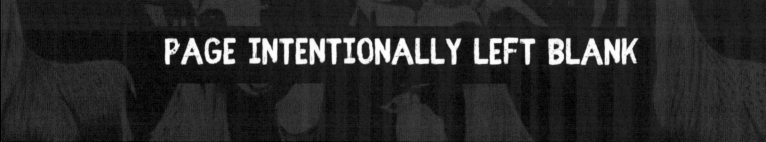

PAGE INTENTIONALLY LEFT BLANK

PAGE INTENTIONALLY LEFT BLANK

PAGE INTENTIONALLY LEFT BLANK

PAGE INTENTIONALLY LEFT BLANK

PAGE INTENTIONALLY LEFT BLANK

PAGE INTENTIONALLY LEFT BLANK

PAGE INTENTIONALLY LEFT BLANK

PAGE INTENTIONALLY LEFT BLANK

PAGE INTENTIONALLY LEFT BLANK

PAGE INTENTIONALLY LEFT BLANK

PAGE INTENTIONALLY LEFT BLANK

PAGE INTENTIONALLY LEFT BLANK

We hope you enjoyed your book from Infinite Creativity Publishing!

.....again...we're writing to ask you a favor - we'd love to get your feedback. We put a lot of work into creating high-quality content & imagery. We love the craft and hope you appreciate it.

Your opinion is super important to us, and we're always looking for ways to improve our products & artwork. So we would be very grateful if you can **please leave us a review on Amazon**! Thank you and have a blessed day.

Also, feel free to visit us at our website available via the QR code below.

Made in the USA
Middletown, DE
22 September 2023

39092306R00075